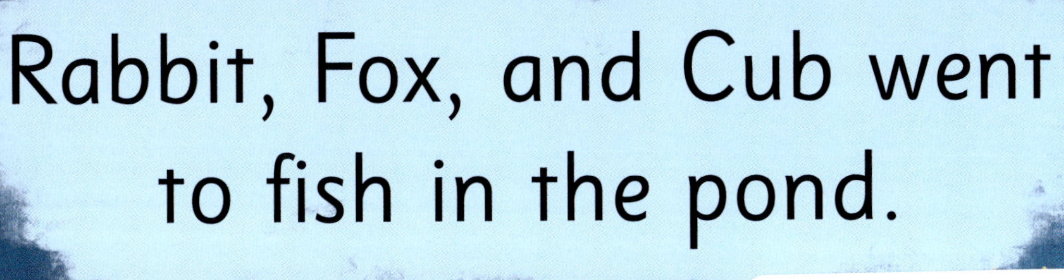

Rabbit, Fox, and Cub went to fish in the pond.

The Moon reflected
on the pond.

Rabbit had a plan
to trick Fox and Cub.

The Moon has landed in the pond, and we cannot fish!

I will get it out with this net.

I will help!

Fox and Cub
fell into the pond
and got wet.

Rabbit giggled as he helped Fox and Cub out of the pond.